Rainn—a novel

Text: Amy Silbergeld & Matthew Landis
Illustrations: Jonas Wessel

F;R:

ISBN: 978-91-980903-2-1
Typographic and other form: Freke Räihä

Rainn

Kathy comes from a good family. But she has no money. She is twenty-six years old, has no job, and holds degrees from good universities in performance art. Kathy has a good body and knows how to act unemotional in social situations. She lives alone in New York City. She used to live in San Francisco and decides to go to San Francisco to visit some friends and a man she has been talking to on the Internet. The man is an artist on the brink of fame and Kathy believes that she is in love with him. Kathy's flight departs on time. She is wearing black jeans and under her jeans is a bit of blood and some pink marks on her thighs because she slashed her legs with a pair of scissors before she left for the airport. Kathy's biggest feeling about the slashes on her legs is humiliation, because she feels like she's done something teenaged and she feels like she's always doing something teenaged. The slashes also hurt and Kathy is afraid she has a personality disorder even though her therapist says that she doesn't. Kathy has a large bag of bulk almonds and she eats them slowly over the length of the flight. She bites them in half and runs her tongue over their smooth middles. There isn't a movie or Internet service and she doesn't have a book with her. She fantasizes vaguely about the man she's been flirting with online, recalling some of their conversations. She can't picture his face in her head even though she's seen lots of pictures of him on the Internet. Kathy feels depressed and hungry when she gets off the plane. She hasn't really eaten anything but almonds in almost a month, which is why she has such a good body. Kathy doesn't think that her body looks good, but other people
7→ do. Kathy thinks that she looks like a sick person, and much older than twenty-six. She buys a coffee in the airport and drinks it while she waits for her friends to come. Kathy's friends Kim and Mickey pick her up in Mickey's Volvo. Kim is cheerful and drinking beer out of a metal water bottle. Mickey is in a bad mood but gives Kathy a hug for the first time and tells her that she really looks like shit.

Kathy says

thank you

and Kim laughs and hands Kathy the water bottle. Kim gives everyone a cigarette and lights them all with a Marilyn Monroe lighter.

Where do you want to go?

Kim asks.

We can go anywhere.

Are there any shows?

Kathy asks.

There is a thing at Dan's house in the backyard,

Kim says.

I don't remember which bands but lots of people will be there.

I want to go to Dan's,

Mickey says.

That's good then,

Kathy says.

Let's go to Dan's later. What kind of bands?

I don't know,

says Kim.

Rockbands probably. We can go to the dyke bar before it's crowded and drink and then go to Oakland for the show.

Will you stop calling it that,

Mickey says.

I'm a dyke,

Kim says.

I'm allowed to call it a dyke bar.

I'm not offended,

Mickey says. 8→

Just annoyed.

Oh, Mickey,

Kim says.

Can we please go to the LESBIAN bar?

Sure,

Mickey says.

They drive to the Mission and Mickey drops Kim and Kathy off in front of the lesbian bar because it will take a long time to park the car. Kathy puts on purple lipstick and hands the lipstick to Kim who also puts some on.

I don't have very much money,

Kathy says.

I have some,

Kim says.

I will buy you drinks and we can just eat at my apartment.

Thanks,

Kathy says. Kathy texts Steven, who is the man she's been talking to on the Internet. Steven lives in the Mission. Kathy tells Steven she is near his house getting drinks. Steven texts back quickly. He says he is nearby, just walking around with a famous writer who Kathy has heard of but never met. Kathy asks Kim if it's fine for Steven and the famous writer to come to the bar. Kim says she has never heard of either of them but that they should definitely come. Kathy tells Steven that he and the famous writer should come to the bar and have drinks. Steven says okay. Kim orders beers and whiskey shots from the very thin and manic-seeming bartender. Kim and Kathy drink very quickly and Kim orders more drinks right away.

I'm so glad you're here,

Kim says.

I love you.

I love you, too,

Kathy says.

9→ I'm having a good time.

Steven and the famous writer sit down at the bar. Steven sits next to Kathy and hugs her and as soon as she smells him she knows she wants to have sex with him. Steven introduces the famous writer to Kathy and Kim. Kim and Steven high five and then improvise a secret handshake. They like each other right away because they are both drunk. The famous writer orders a Coke and Steven orders more beers and whiskies. Kathy has already had several drinks but cannot get drunk. Steven puts his hand on Kathy's thigh.

I fucking love you,

Steven says to Kathy.

I'm going to fucking marry you and lock you in a cage.

The famous writer examines Kathy's figure and orders an expensive beer. The bar is not crowded. There are only a few other people in the bar.

You have a good body,

the famous writer says to Kathy.

Are you kidding me,

Steven says.

She's fucking hot.

It's a very good body,

the famous writer says to Kathy. Kim doesn't feel jealous and smiles genuinely at Kathy and winks at her in a cartoonish manner. Mickey shows up looking frustrated but doesn't complain about parking. He introduces himself to the famous writer.

Steven,

he says to Steven.

Oh, right,

Steven says.

Mickey. How do you know everyone. How do you know Kathy.

We met six or seven years ago,

Mickey says.

We met through music stuff.

The three of us had a band once, 10→

Kim says.

I've known Mickey since high school. We're both from Palo Alto.

The famous writer says that he's from Palo Alto and he and Mickey and Kim talk about Palo Alto. Kathy says she needs a cigarette and Kim gives her one and Steven follows Kathy outside. He touches her body over her clothes. She lights her cigarette and he takes it from her and puts it out with his fingers and puts it in his pack pocket. He kisses Kathy and they make out in front of the lesbian bar. There are lots of people out, walking to dinner and shopping. Steven rubs Kathy's crotch through her jeans. He rubs her thighs and she flinches.

Come to Oakland tonight,

Kathy says.

You can come in the car. We're going to a show.

Okay,

Steven says.

Can I wear what I'm wearing or should I put on a nicer shirt or something? You look fucking great.

It's a house show,

Kathy says.

It doesn't matter. Do you promise that you're coming?

Are you kidding,

Steven says.

I want to be inside of you the whole time you're here.

His voice is faggy. He has an erection and gives Kathy her cigarette back.

I want to be on top of you all the time,

he says.

I want to make you cum. You look like you don't eat anything.

I've been sort of depressed,

Kathy says.

I feel better now that I'm here.

I'll buy you drugs,

Steven says.

11→ Can I buy you drugs?

Sure,

Kathy says.

I'm tired.

Oh sweetie,

he says.

You had a long flight. I'll buy you some coke and we can go to Oakland and do coke together and fuck.

Okay,

Kathy says.

I hate coke, but okay.

They go back into the lesbian bar and Steven tells everyone that he needs to buy some cocaine. The famous writer says that he needs to meet someone for dinner and whispers something in Steven's ear and tells Kim and Mickey that it was nice talking to them and pokes Kathy in the stomach. Steven buys everyone else more drinks and calls his coke dealer and asks if he can pick up an eight ball, loudly, and no one in the bar seems to mind. Steven says that his coke dealer will meet them at the bar and Kim and Steven high five. Kathy drinks four more whiskeys but still doesn't feel drunk. She is smaller than Steven and Mickey and much smaller than Kim but they are all drunk and Kathy can't get drunk. She knows she should offer to drive the car but she doesn't feel like it so she goes to the bathroom and puts on more purple lipstick. She unbuttons her jeans and looks at her legs and splashes water from the toilet onto them. She finds face powder in her bag and tries to apply it to her legs but decides it isn't the right color and rinses it off with toilet water and pulls her jeans back up without drying her legs. Her jeans get a bit damp and she looks in the mirror and sucks in her cheeks and doesn't look much different when she sucks in her cheeks. She messes her hair up a little bit and checks her teeth for lipstick in the mirror and tries to look at her face like she's someone else and says the word STUPID several times to herself. She puts her hand down her jeans to make sure her cunt is shaved even though she knows it's shaved. She shakes her head quickly to see if it makes her feel drunk but she doesn't feel drunk. Kathy slams the bathroom door on the way out and Steven has his arm around Kim and his feet on Mickey's lap. Mickey was making a miserable face.

I got you some drugs,

Steven says.

Thanks,

Kathy says.

I really hate coke. I wasn't kidding.

I love coke,

Kim says.

No one is doing any drugs in my car,

Mickey says.

I don't care if you do drugs but please don't do any drugs in my car.

They all go to Steven's apartment where a group thin girls are drinking beer in the kitchen. Steven introduces the thin girls to Kathy and her friends and asks the thin girls if they want to do some coke. The girls all say okay and Steven cuts thick lines of coke on a cookbook. Everyone other than Mickey does a line of coke.

Want to see my bedroom.

Steven says to Kathy.

Yeah,

Kathy says.

Can we do more coke?

Of course,

says Steven.

You are so fucking hot. You have such narrow shoulders. You look like you're twelve.

He guides Kathy into his bedroom by the waist. Steven
kisses Kathy on the neck and pushes her hard onto his
bed and she just stays on the bed. He takes his keys and
a bag of coke out of his pocket and gives Kathy a key
bump. Kathy doesn't feel tired anymore but she doesn't
feel high, either. Steven gets on the bed and puts his
13→ hand down Kathy's pants and starts rubbing her clit.

You don't have any books in your room,

Kathy says.

Where are all your books?

Some of them are in the living room. I sold the rest of them because I didn't have any money.

I just want to stay here. I think I'm fucked if I stay in New York. Let me just stay here with you.

That's perfect. I fucking love you. We can never leave my room. Or I can get you a job at Kink if you want and they'll pay you whatever you want because you're so fucking hot.

I have too many tattoos. They want girl-next-door types. No one wants to see me get beat up.

I do,

Steven says.

I want to watch you get the shit beat out of you and watch you get fucked.

They don't hire you if you have too many tattoos.

Kim comes in and Steven keeps rubbing Kathy's clit.

Do you want to go to the show soon, guys,

Kim says.

Yeah,

Kim says.

Okay.

Do I look okay, Kim,

Steven asks.

You look hot,

Kim says.

Let's go in ten minutes or something, and we're all drinking your beer, Steven.

I love you,

Steven says.

No,

Kim says,

I love you. Both of you. Can I see your cock?

Steven pulls his cock out of his jeans. It is long and semi hard. Kim starts laughing.

Are you laughing at my cock, 14→

Steven says.

Yeah,

Kim says, and she leaves the room laughing harder and harder. Steven starts rubbing Kathy's clit really hard. She takes his hand out of her pants and says they should go to the show.

15→

Looking in the window Alexina asks Abel,

Why don't I have a clitoris?

Abel replies,

We were not designed for sex to function as a mode of pleasure.

Alexina is surprised.

Is that what pleasure looks like for them?

Abel chuckles. Abel drops the piece of apple core it had been holding and stares for a moment at a peanut shell and then looks back in the window.

Pleasure is a complicated emotion. For them, pleasure is cleaved together, whether to guilt, or shame, or joy, or excitement, or confusion, and even sometimes all of these things at once. What the one having her clitoris rubbed is experiencing is probably not pleasure. Look at her face.

Alexina looks at hard into the window at her. Then she looks at Abel.

What's a face?

Abel sighs and continues speaking as if Abel had never given her room to interject.

The experience of sexual pleasure is miraculous,

Abel begins.

It is not the only thing that is miraculous, but that is the adjective which should be described to it. There is one of Them, named Georges Bataille, who once compared the climax of sexual pleasure to 'a little death' and thus the return to the body from ekstasis or from distraction or whatever you wish to call it is always a miniature resurrection, a small, insignificant Easter morning.

Alexina blinks at Abel. Abel continues.

The climax is the obliteration of individual consciousness, of self-consciousness. The climax is the ultimate forgetting followed by the rush of remembrance. The neurotransmitters that flood their brains are invading Visigoths competing for limited real estate and the climax is the breach of 16→
the gate. How could it be anything but miraculous? How do they survive it?

They are both silent, looking into the window at Kathy and Steven. Steven is sulking as he puts his cock back into his pants. Kathy begins to button her pants. Steven says something quietly. They know because Kathy picks up her head. Her face is blank. She says something back to Steven. Steven shrugs his shoulders and looks for something on the floor. Alexina asks Abel,

Did she climax?

No,

Abel replies.

Why, is her clitoris broken?,

Alexina asks.

Abel ignores her as she starts to speak again.

Why is th—

All the same it is miraculous!

Alexina picks up the piece of apple core Abel dropped and sniffs it.

The miraculous need not be ecstatic. No. Not at all. The miraculous can be found anywhere for us, but not for them. They need miracles too much to believe in them.

So what is the miraculous? Or where is the miraculous?,

Alexina asks Abel. Abel takes a deep breath and hurriedly scoops up the peanut shell and chews around the edges before tossing it aside. Abel speaks hurriedly.

The seat of the miraculous is a vomit green couch, rain-beaten and musty on the side of the road. It is what we uncover in basements. The miraculous is forgotten. The miraculous is not even silent, it is screaming and ignored. The miraculous is timid when cast over by flashlight. The keen, sharp, exacting light of analysis cannot shine through the murky pool of the miraculous. The depths of the miraculous are black or deep dark browns and green at best. We feel its mud ooze between our toes and laugh as the tide spirits away the sand beneath our feet. It is miraculous to sink with the the outgoing tide.

He looks back at the window again and notices that Kathy and Steven are no longer in the room. Alexina looks at Abel and asks,

17→ What do we do now?

Over here,

Abel replies, scurrying along the ledge of the building around to the front where he can hear them all speaking. Alexina follows Abel.

Kathy suddenly high and talking and talking, the sun seeming to drop directly down, just down, Kathy feeling like her cunt is attached to her body.

All we do is need,

she says.

What have I done for art? I haven't done anything so it's for nothing that everyone thinks I'm crazy. I'm not emotional about it and really honestly I don't care what I've done or if people think anything or even if they don't and am I the only one who doesn't want attention anymore I mean I wish I didn't look like anything to anyone I didn't want but for fuck's sake I am not emotional I am just not an emotional person I think I like coke again and Steven I think you're so smart and you can do anything you want but I'm not smart anymore and fuck I'm happy for myself.

Mickey rolls his eyes and Kim tells Kathy to shut up because Kathy has the most feelings of anyone.

I fucking love you when you're sloppy,

Steven says.

You have lipstick on your teeth and it's fucking hot do you know how much I love you.

Then they are in Mickey's car driving over the Bay Bridge listening to Pavement which is Mickey's choice. Then they are at Dan's and Steven gives Kathy and Kim the bag of coke and they go to the bathroom and Kim cuts thick messy lines with her library card on the counter.

You can trust me,

Kim says to Kathy.

You don't have to be so fucking contained so tell me anything I'm so good at listening and I know you're sad.

I'm having a good time,

Kathy says.

I'm a whore though and I guess some of them treat me okay but I use men for money the way my mother used men for money and I always said I wouldn't take their money I always said it was too easy but what else can I do. My mom was a whore and now I'm a whore. Jesus I just want someone to like me.

Steven likes you,

Kim says.

That's not what makes you not a whore. I feel like I'm in a movie. I know how gross and American that is I swear but I can't make the feeling stop.

Bands start Kathy is fucked up but won't admit it to herself Steven finds her outside drags her in by her wrist takes her to a mostly-empty room with a desk and a desktop computer on it, some stacks of books. He lifts he pushes her against the wall her legs wrap around him she tries to pull his cock into her she wants his cum he cums fast slamming her against the wall then bends her over and some of his cum drips down her leg and he finger fucks her cunt and ass. She spasms her cunt and ass squeezing his fingers.

I'm pretending I'm someone else,

Steven says.

What,

Kathy says.

Pretending you're getting molested by some other guy behind my back,

he says. Surfy noise music from outside, Kathy thinking we are stuck as a generation we are stuck on a personal level fingers fucking me Steven's fingers fucking me I'm in love with someone else but I don't know who we are so fucked.

You should make some porn at Kink,

Steven says.

You can rape people like that you can rape people with that cycle of arousal and rejection.

I don't want to rape anyone,

Kathy says.

You don't actually love me.

I fucking love you so shut the fuck up.

19→ She cums again he takes his fingers out and puts them in her mouth she thinks I am so fucked.

Alexina and Abel could not follow Them. They are afraid of cars. Alexina and Abel ran along telephone wires. They sneak into a dumpster behind a pizza place and Alexina asks Abel to help her find her clitoris. Abel explains that Alexina does not have one. Alexina tells Abel to fuck her anyway. Abel says that Its cock does not fuck as well as Abel's cunt. Alexina says she doesn't care. Abel fucks her, Abel's flaccid penis languidly slipping out of her each time Abel pulls her haunches back. Alexina says forget it, so Abel does. They fall asleep in the dumpster. They dream. This is what they dreamed.

20→

Four months ago. Steven tells Kathy to write her name on pages of his book with her shit and period blood and her cunt otherwise and she refuses to write her name in shit. Four years ago. Kathy is sure love exists she knows it she will do anything to have it and it makes her feel like a needy child tantruming she literally breaks windows with her fists a few times always abandoned buildings at night she has not lived in New York long she is looking for love she wants it and she will get fucked however she has to be tough if she has to is weak she feels weak knowing she just wants love. Kathy wakes up to the baby next door crying early and the sun is just coming up, too fast it seems, rolling into the sky over New York City like a hot marble. I am not a successful person Kathy thinks. She makes coffee and drinks it and doesn't clean up after herself and she takes a shit and doesn't shower and makes a piece of toast and butters the toast and eats it standing up. Kathy calls her mother who is awake because she has a very early exercise class.

I am not a successful person,

Kathy says to her mother.

It is a bad economy,

her mother says.

No one has a job. All your friends are unemployed or have unpaid internships and no one has money now you didn't do anything wrong.

I feel like I did,

Kathy says.

Should I get married I don't know what to do I don't want to die can I have some money.

Kathy's mother says she'll give Kathy some money later.

21→ Don't ask again this month.

Kathy's mother says.

I will never be successful.

Kathy says. Kathy has no job, just an unpaid internship with a publisher of art books. It is Thursday so she doesn't go to the publisher and has no plans other than to try not to spend much money and to leave her apartment and not just sleep all day. She calls her drug dealer and arranges to buy some drugs with the money her mother is giving her. She needs to go to West Harlem to buy the drugs so she thinks she might as well make her way uptown slowly over a few hours. Kathy buys an expensive coffee in Chelsea and drinks it very slowly and it gets cold. Kathy buys a scarf from a table on the street because it's getting cold. The scarf is grey and burgundy and made of a blend synthetic fabrics. It feels soft but also cheap and Kathy walks faster because she thinks she should get some slightly vigorous exercise because it's supposed to be good for depression. Soon she is on the Upper West Side and outside of a diner, there she sees an acquaintance who she knows through a friend from graduate school. Her acquaintance is named Wes and he is in a band that has maintained its popularity for a decade though Kathy does not like the band.

22→

Abel begins to talk in Its sleep. Abel begins to dream history, to dream the past. Abel dreams Kathy and dreams Kim and dreams Steven and dreams Mickey and dreams Pavement and dreams a car and dreams the Golden Gate Bridge and dreams BART and dreams guns and dreams cocaine and dreams Wes and dreams hard cocks and wet cunts and dreams what it feels like to cum and dreams eyebrows and dreams success and dreams money and dreams Alexina and dreams dreams that dream history, dream the past, dream Kathy, dream Kim... In Its dream Abel hears a voice and the voice sounds like a man that Its father told Abel about once. Its father told Abel that the man was not a man that he had ever seen but Its great great great grandfather had known. This man lived here in San Francisco. This man died here in San Francisco. The man died when he was shot by a psychotic Catholic. Abel has a brief moment of lucidity in Its dream. Abel wonders if It is a psychotic Catholic because It is hearing a dead man's voice in Its dream. But Abel buries this thought. Abel doesn't want to lose the dream. Abel can't remember the man's name. The man says that's not important. Abel figures he would know best. Abel cannot see the man but he sees Kathy in New York City buying a grey and burgundy scarf. The man tells Abel that even faggots can be misogynists. Abel asks the man why he's telling It that. The man replies that even intersexed squirrels can be misogynists. Abel feels offended. Abel is incredulous. Too incredulous to speak. The man tsk-tsk's at Abel. The man tells Abel that Kathy is not a signifier, she is a human being. Abel
23→ asks if human beings do not signify. The man says that they do. So, Abel beings to say but the man interrupts. Sex is not miraculous, the man says, it is violence. The man goes on. The man says that men of his time had to fuck other men in the bushes of Central Park, at truck stops, in the bathrooms of special bars, in quiet cold water flats while listening to Mahler and bossa nova, in the backs of oversized tanks of cars like Plymouths and Chryslers. The man talks about men and boys being

fucked and raped in prisons and schools and churches. About the epidemic of AIDS in minority communities because of the prevalence of IV drug users. About the epidemic of AIDS amongst gays because of God's cruel sense of humor. He tells Abel about unspeakable horror. Of human sacrifice. He tells Abel about a boy in Wyoming who was tethered to a barbed wire fence, beaten to the brink of death and then left there to die alone because he liked putting other men's cocks in his mouth and was not afraid to admit that this was the case. Abel listens to all of these stories. The man asks Abel if It still thinks sex is miraculous. Abel says Abel doesn't know. The man replies that sex is psychic genocide, that an entire generation has been taught to commodify sex, that there has been such a leveling down of creative potential and human freedom that people assume that the inherent lack of freedom, choice and subjective agency they experience is codified in their own sexual behavior. He tells Abel about the market of human sexuality, the way it gets traded around the arcane hierarchy of suffering and explains how everyone is in the hierarchy, even Abel. He explains how sex gets up in front of culture like Marx's table and dances and proves not only its utility but the veracity of its capacity to engender an exchange, and exchange which is almost always an inequity, almost always a form of violence. The man tells Abel that another man like him once said something that Abel should remember. The man tells Abel what the other man said. It was that we have since become an extraordinarily confessing society. Confession has spread its effects far and wide: in the judicial system, in medicine, in pedagogy, in familial 24→
relations, in amorous relationships, in everyday life and in the most solemn rituals; crimes are confessed, sins are confessed, thoughts and desires are confessed, one's past and one's dreams are confessed, one's childhood is confessed; one's diseases and problems are confessed. The man told Abel that desire was nothing more than the internalization of the compulsion to confess, that satisfying desire was satisfying the need to confess. The

man told Abel that people have spent their whole lives trying not to feel in order to never have to relieve the fear and uncertainty they've encountered in the world in the past 11 years. The man told Abel that the sad part about irony was that irony was sad. The man told Abel that he was unnecessary. The man told Abel that he had fucked Guy Debord in heaven. The man told Abel that Guy Debord's cock tasted like piss and whiskey. The man told Abel that until It took Guy Debord's cock in Its mouth It could never be a prophet. Abel told the man It didn't want to be a prophet, that It didn't want to put Guy Debord's cock in Its mouth. Abel woke up, gagging.

The man told Abel that emotions were difficult to feel.

Hi,

Wes says to Kathy.

What are you doing here.

I don't know,

says Wes.

I guess I'm on a walk. My girlfriend lives uptown and I slept there. We are in a fight and if I were a different type of person I would hit her because she just won't listen.

I'm sorry,

Kathy says.

I am on a walk and once I get the money for it I'm going to buy some drugs and you can come if you want are you hungry I haven't eaten.

He says he hasn't eaten either so they go to the diner because it's right there and the food is very cheap.

Are you a vegetarian,

Kathy says and Wes says

No are you,

and Kathy says

No.

They order food and coffee.

My girlfriends think I'm a misogynist,

Wes says.

I don't think I am a misogynist I just don't know what it's like to be a woman.

Do you think women are people,

Kathy says.

Yes,

Wes says.

Then you are a feminist, 26→

Kathy says,

and she is probably wrong but what did you say that made her unhappy.

I said she was being aggressive and that I didn't like that. She is an aggressive person and it's not about gender it's about aggression when I haven't done anything I mean I haven't done anything wrong.

Yeah,

Kathy says,

I am afraid when someone gets aggressive and I want everyone to treat me very gently or I become upset. I am easily upset I think. I don't think that's a gender thing really I just think I'm a depressed person and also sensitive.

It is better to be sensitive than hard,

Wes says.

At least you are not hard. My girlfriend is hard and prides herself in being hard and she doesn't just do it in a bad neighborhood at night she does it with me and with everyone and she can't turn it off.

Do you mean she is tough,

Kathy says.

No,

Wes says,

I mean she is hard and cold and wants people to be afraid of her because lots of bad things happened to her.

Oh like she was raped,

Kathy says.

No,

Wes says.

She was never raped but she never knew her father and her mom was a drug addict and she's never had any money and she has back problems.

Were you ever raped,

Kathy says.

No,

says Wes.

But women have made me feel uncomfortable because they think that they can just touch me sexually but they can't.

You're right,

Kathy says.

That isn't okay. I'm sorry to hear that.

27→ Have you been raped,

Wes says.

Yeah,

Kathy says.

It was date rape I guess and I don't feel traumatized or anything just a little mad. It was a pretty long time ago and I'm okay now I mean I'm not okay but I'm okay about that.

I'm sorry that happened,

Wes said.

I'm glad it feels resolved or how should I put it. It's good that you are okay I mean not okay but okay about what happened to you.

How old are you,

Kathy says.

I'm exactly ten years older than you probably,

Wes says.

I am thirty-four.

I am twenty-two,

says Kathy.

So you are not ten years older you are older than that even. Do you feel old.

I don't know what that means,

Wes says.

You're not a woman,

says Kathy.

I have to go. I have to go get drugs soon do you want to come.

Are you a junky or something,

Wes says.

You look sort of like a junky.

That's a shitty thing to say. I don't know what you mean and no, I need to go pick up some pot I don't do drugs other than pot and occasionally MDMA or blow or something but hardly ever and I can't even afford to be a junky, I don't have any money.

I just meant you're skinny most girls like that,

Wes says.

That's really fucked and do you mean you're trying to have sex with me,

Kathy says.

No,

says Wes. 28→

I mean I think you're an attractive person. Do you think I'm attractive?

Kathy rolls her eyes and drinks coffee. Do you want to come with me she says because you can come uptown with me and get this pot and we can smoke pot.

Sure,

Wes says.

I don't care what I do.

What do you mean you don't care what you do,

Kathy says.

I don't know what I mean,

says Wes.

Let's go get your drugs. You should have said weed, now it seems like you wanted me to think you're a junky.

I don't care what you think about me,

Kathy says.

Do you have a boyfriend,

Wes says.

What the fuck,

says Kathy.

You don't have to answer,

Wes says.

You're annoyed by my uterine fury,

Kathy says.

I love women and I think they are people you're trying to trap me I'm sorry I have a cock,

Wes says.

No you aren't,

says Kathy.

Yeah I want to have a cock,

Wes says.

You shouldn't comment on anyone's weight,

says Kathy.

It's not okay, it makes me angry I'm not skinny anyway not in New York and I bet your girlfriend weighs 90 pounds.

Something like that, she is about as big as you,

29→ he says.

I am not 90 pounds I am much more,

says Kathy.

I once met a guy on a fetish website and he liked BDSM stuff and I wanted to get held down you know but he kept almost killing me I mean really and it didn't seem like an accident. He was acting out his hatred of women and he encouraged me to diet he wanted me to be small. I looked at his computer I thought he was cheating on me and I was miserable and he wasn't cheating but he had child porn on there I mean young girls not toddlers or anything but they all looked around twelve and I can't even remember what exactly the pictures were because I've blocked them out they were horrible and I threw up on his bed and he beat me. It's not that I don't want to be beat up because maybe I do but not like that I didn't call the police. I have to get my pot now there is no way I'll get uptown by then.

Wes pays for the food and pays for a yellow cab and gives Kathy money and waits outside in the cab and Kathy gets her pot. He gives the driver an address in the West Village. What Kathy says:

I mean where is that where are we going now.

My apartment,

Wes says.

Is that okay. I mean do you want to come to my apartment.

Are you trying to fuck me,

Kathy says.

Jesus,

Wes says.

What do you mean.

I mean do you want to put your cock in me what else can I mean,

Kathy says. Kathy thinks she isn't seeming tough enough or smart enough she's still smart enough to seem smart but she just keeps talking and he wants tough and smart she thinks I know it she thinks no one will ever love me I am not a successful person my father didn't love me it's a classic case of whatever I am pathetic and this thinking is so reductive I can't stop talking something is wrong with me I want to be fucked I want to be loved and I'll do anything I have to I'll do anything I'm a baby a big huge fat baby who just wants and wants it's repulsive 30→
and indecent I am an out of control person. Wes slides his arm behind Kathy's waist and she puts her head on his shoulder and turns her head and kisses his neck and thinks I am so stupid I am so fucking stupid. He grabs her jaw hard and kisses her with his lips and tongue and runs his hands through her hair and tucks her hair behind her ears and pulls away and looks at her and she wants to cry and is scared she will so she

kisses him and feels around for his cock which is hard and she rubs it through his jeans and he cups her cunt with his hands to see if it feels warm and it does. Wes lives in a second floor walkup and he brings her inside and closes the door and pushes her against it and her skull bangs against the door and he presses his pelvis into hers and he pushes her onto the floor and takes her clothes off and she just stares at him and then asks him to touch her and he doesn't touch her with his hands or even take his clothes off he just unbuttons his jeans and takes his cock out and he's over her running the head of his hard cock against her clit and slipping it into her cunt without asking her. As soon as he pushes inside her she cums and she feels crazy he fucks her hard and she pushes herself against him and he holds her down by her arms and her body is breaking she knows it she has spinal damage she's cumming again and this time he can tell because her cunt contracts so tight and then soft and he doesn't seem to care he keeps fucking her hard and she's cumming again saying

I love you I love you I love you

and he pulls his cock out and cums on her stomach and he rubs his cum into her stomach and he spits on her face and she starts crying.

Did you not like it,

he says.

I love you,

she says.

No you don't you just came a lot you'll be fine,

he says.

31→ Do you like me,

she says.

Shut up,

he says and he goes to the bathroom and she can hear him shitting. Kathy keeps crying and can't stop crying.

Stop crying,

Wes says.

Jesus.

I love you,

she says

and you don't even like me why do I always do this to myself I'm so stupid.

Are you fucking kidding me,

he says.

You need to stop. Let's smoke and you need to calm down will that calm you down.

The pot is in his pocket she puts her clothes on there is money in the pocket with the pot she takes the pot and the money and he knows she's taking it and she clutches it in a fist and slams his door and puts on sunglasses and cries while she walks home which isn't far and she counts the money when she gets home and there are ten twenties and she stops crying and counts them a few times and falls asleep even though it's bright out and sleeps all day and through the night. The next day she calls Wes who of course doesn't answer and she keeps calling and finally he answers it's later he's been out of town for a funeral he says she tells him part of her soul is gone he tells her she can't possibly believe in souls she says you're right it's my brain my brain is breaking and breaking. He starts to think he has taken part of her soul and can feel it clinging to him in his apartment holding an ankle and he tries to shake it off but it keeps on with the horrible sounds like a large animal dying. She gets fucked for money every day for six days and on the seventh day she rests.

32→

Alexina asks Abel if Abel is okay. Abel nods while continuing to cough and retch. Alexina rubs Its back. Abel looks back at her standing on Its hind legs wobbling. Abel leans agains the slimy metal of the dumpster and Its insides heave and starts to vomit. Abel belches and spits, trying to get the test of the dumpster out of Its mouth.

Not me,

Abel says.

I'm not even here.

The last band that plays at Dan's is one of Kathy's old boyfriend's band. She doesn't want to see him or hear his voice even.

I have to leave,

Kathy says.

I don't want to be here and my friends will want to stay all night. I need more coke or we need to leave or both.

Come to my house and I'll feed you Xanax and hold you like a fucking baby,

Steven says.

Okay,

Kathy says.

BART probably isn't running.

I'll call a cab right now I want to get you a cab and take care of you and watch you sleep in my bed.

Okay,

Kathy says.

Yeah.

Steven feeding Kathy Xanax with his mouth. She doesn't know how much. It must be early. He undresses her and wraps her in a blanket and puts her on his bed. Kathy's hands stop shaking, her limbs relax, her heartbeat slows maybe too much she worries as much as she can about her heartbeat which isn't very much.

There's no plot,

she says.

I just do the same things over again. There isn't a narrative. I haven't learned anything. I've been the same way, I keep being the same way. I can't derive any meaning from this. Where is the story here? I meet someone who wants to treat me like a child or a whore or a child whore and
I'll go anywhere and do anything for it when it's just whoring. 34→

I love you,

Steven says.

I want to be inside you all the time.

It's a performance and that's fine,

she says.

Everyone does it and maybe you do it more than some people but it doesn't make you less real of a person than anyone else. Do you exist when you're alone?

Steven takes long underwear from a pile of clothes and dresses her slowly.

Kathy,

he says.

We've been getting fucked up all day. I'm old enough to be your father. You are a child but you're smart and I've never treated you like you aren't. The fantasy stuff is sexual. The performance is a sex thing. You are in my real bed and I'm listening to you.

I'm sorry,

Kathy says. She starts to cry.

You're okay. Do you want me to be your friend? Is that what you want? I don't know what you want but I thought we were having fun and I'm not trying to hurt you.

He runs his hands over her legs.

Shit,

she says. Her cuts are infected, maybe from the toilet water.

You're young and you're not half as ruined as you think you are.

I can't stop being teenaged. My brain stopped developing. There's something wrong with me and I don't know what it is. I guess I'm glad I got stupid, I'm sure it's easier, why are you being so nice to me.

Are you tired yet.

I'm exhausted and I need to start eating more tomorrow or I'm going to die of a heart attack.

You can sleep. I will feed you tomorrow.

He takes his clothes off and gets into his bed with her and pulls her towards him.

You can fuck me if you want,

Kathy says.

35→ Kathy,

Steven says.

It's okay to just sleep.

He holds her. His cock is hard against her ass and she falls asleep and he falls asleep.

Steven is almost a teenager. He lives in a small town in Southern California and has never left. His parents are poor. His mother is severely bipolar and jabs him with the heels of her shoes when she's angry. His father does some kind of work for the military and that's all Steven knows about his father. Steven's father comes home every evening with a six pack of cheap Mexican lager and drinks it and reads the local newspaper at the kitchen table. No one makes dinner for Steven but there is a jar of quarters and dimes on the counter and Steven buys candy bars which he walks two miles to buy. His teeth and gums hurt and no one takes him to the dentist. His cousin Natalie comes to stay with Steven and his parents because her parents kicked her out. She is five years older than Steven. She sleeps with him in his twin bed. Natalie shows Steven what sex is and Steven thinks he is in love with her. He doesn't tell her he just lets her fuck him. He has weak orgasms and knows even then she is using his body to get herself off but he thinks he is in love with her. She buys a radio and they listen to popular music. Every love song is about Steven and Natalie, Steven thinks. He cries when she turns eighteen and moves to Los Angeles. She wants to be famous and she doesn't care what for. She writes Steven short letters for a while. He gets old enough to understand that she has hurt him badly. Natalie has a boyfriend who is older. Natalie takes her clothes off and has her picture taken. Natalie sticks her tongue in another women's mouth and someone takes their picture. Natalie takes one cock in her ass and another in her cunt and someone takes a picture. Natalie's boyfriend drives to Steven's town when Natalie dies of a drug overdose. Steven is physically strong for the last time in his life and he punches the man in the face and the man is on the floor holding his face and this is in the living room and Steven's mother is in a hospital and his father is fucking a woman he works with. Steven kicks the man's head into the wall until the man starts bleeding out of his mouth and Steven tells him to get the fuck out or he'll kill the

man he tells the man I will fucking kill you. The man leaves and Steven never sees him again. Steven doesn't go to Natalie's funeral.   Steven moves to San Francisco when he turns seventeen. He meets a famous feminist writer a few years later. Steven works in at a magazine where he makes copies and transcribes interviews. He wants to go to school. He meets the famous feminist writer at a party for the magazine. He's been invited because he's likable and sells drugs. The writer has very short blonde hair and large tattoos on her back. She is muscular but small. She approaches Steven and they talk and she likes him right away because he's smart. She is the first person he tells about Natalie. Steven moves in with the famous feminist writer. He is happy to watch her write and bring her things. She likes to be pinned down and hit when they fuck and Steven likes pinning her down and hitting her. He doesn't feel sick afterwards because he knows she is powerful. She has cancer in one of her breasts. Steven changes his name to Steven from what it was before and moves out and the famous feminist writer leaves the country and dies of breast cancer. Steven starts hunting women like they are stupid animals. He knows he's doing it and if he feels anything he feels proud of himself. He never rapes or hits a woman but he is manipulative and he seeks out the weak and insecure. He dates women who are younger than him. He dates the most beautiful women only. If he thinks anything it's that he isn't doing wrong because their beauty is a type of power he will never have. If he thinks anything it's that he's ruined and he'll never
37→ leave California in his life and he'll never have any money and he'll never love anyone in any way for any reason because love means your body as something to grind against and your body means dying and you have less control over your body than you think. He'll never love anyone because we have less control over our bodies than we think.   Stevens parents are dead. He sometimes thinks I am an orphan but doesn't cry. He writes a novel and the reaction is mixed. One review says that Steven

believes that all women are weak. But Steven believes that all people are weak. He starts writing strong women with every kind of power and weak impotent men. The reviews are overwhelmingly positive. He makes some money and visits New York and London and Paris. He rents and furnishes an apartment in San Francisco. He can't cum if he doesn't imagine being one of many men in a gangbang, fucking a vague memory of the famous feminist writer almost to death.

Kathy looks like the famous feminist writer would have if the famous feminist writer had been groomed by her mother. Kathy has the same light hair which is the color it is specifically so it can be as close to no color as hair can be. Kathy's hair is long, she has loose curls and naturally bowed lips and is almost conventionally attractive but sometimes too thin for even that and tired looking also and too Jewish in the face which the famous feminist writer was also. Kathy also has cancer in one of her breasts but she doesn't know she has cancer. Steven isn't lying when he says he loves her, at least he believes he isn't lying even if he's acting faggy and performing everything he says to her even performing when he says I love you. He feels afraid all the time, afraid of everyone but he doesn't feel afraid of Kathy. He wants to give her everything but he doesn't have very much money and he doesn't think she will stay with him and if she does she will die and if she doesn't she will die. She sleeps late and he touches her hair and tries to think of things he can do for her that don't cost very much money. He stupidly buys her flowers thinking the whole time that it's stupid and that she won't like them. They are spray roses, sort of orange, and he puts them on the bed next to her like her body is a grave. He rests the flowers against her and arranges them so they angle the right way against her waist. He makes coffee and drinks some and wants to wake Kathy up and bring her some but he lets her sleep. Kathy's mother is sort of brain dead from taking so much acid and her mother's mother is demented and hates women more than any man ever could
39→ and Kathy's grandmother's mother died in the Holocaust.
Kathy is nine and breaks her arm. Her mother says I wish I could feel the pain instead of you. Kathy's mother is fourteen and her mother is telling her she looks cheap. Kathy's grandmother is a happy baby in her mother's arms in Poland and Kathy's grandmother's mother is happy, so happy, the thought of death is impossible, only good things will happen, things are so simple, there is enough to eat and the baby is healthy and barely cries.

She is the happiest baby. Kathy wakes up and Steven is sitting next to her drinking coffee and she asks for some. She finishes it and Steven takes the cup and fills it with more coffee and brings it back to Kathy.

I will give you everything,

Steven says.

I love you and I want to give you everything. Tell me what you've always wanted.

Kathy is spitting her fingers and taking her mascara off with her spit.

What do you mean,

she says.

What have you always wanted,

Steven says.

I guess I'm always watching gangbang porn and I've never done that. It seemed scary for a long time but now I don't know. I've had some threesomes and they were okay but it's a different thing I think. Is that what you meant.

Steven doesn't know what he meant so he guesses he can give Kathy a gangbang.

Who do you want to gangbang you,

Steven says.

I like women sometimes I mean I've fucked women and been fucked by them but if I'm going to be gangbanged I will be gangbanged by men. Otherwise it doesn't have any appeal at all.

I will give you a gangbang,

Steven says as he pins her legs back and licks and sucks her clit.

Things Kathy is worried her family will find in her apartment if she dies in a plane crash or commits suicide include:

One Hitachi Magic Wand vibrator, not recently cleaned.

Two cheap bullet vibrators, not recently cleaned but also not recently used.

Four dildos of varying lengths and girths, not recently cleaned, one unused.

Several dozen suicide notes, only one of them angry and most of them very short, all unfinished and unsigned.

About $20,000 (retail value) worth of designer clothing and accessories, most items stolen from Kathy's mother but some stolen from stores.

Several thousand pornographic images (.jpg files), most of them including one or more of the following:

Gangbangs.

Threesomes (two men, one woman).

Double penetration.

Hardcore BDSM (male dominants, female submissives).

Dollification.

CMNF (Clothed Male Naked Female).

Almost one hundred pieces of poorly written erotica found on the Internet and copy-pasted into .doc files, most of the stories featuring one or more of the following:

Incest (father/daughter).

Forced intercourse (rape), either:

Forced gangbang (gang rape, female victims).

Or.

Forced intercourse (male rapists, female victims).

Unconditional love and acceptance, manifesting as one or more of the following:

Bedwetting (female bedwetter, male sexual partner).

41→ Terminal illness (female patient, male partner).

Romantic love.

Moldy food and other unsanitary conditions.

Steven sat on the front steps of the house after kicking the man in the head and making him leave. He panted exaggeratedly, less from exertion then from excitement. He felt sad but he also felt empowered. He knew that when he told the man I will kill you, he meant it. He knew that he was capable of doing it. Steven is not a psychopath. Steven is aware that what he does is wrong. That what he thinks is wrong. That his existence is all wrong. But Steven does these things anyway because he hates himself. He punishes himself by indulging his own worst ideas about himself.   If Steven smoked, he would smoke, he thinks. Steven doesn't smoke. As he sits in the steps he notices a squirrel regarding him, curiously. The squirrel doesn't look like other squirrels. The squirrel sits on the edge of the lawn, still. Not chattering or scurrying. Just sitting. Steven picks up a small stone off the ground near the steps and throws it at the squirrel. The stone is light and does not travel far and the squirrel does not move. Then the squirrel walks closer. Steven throws another small stone. The squirrel does not move as it sails over his head.   The tyranny of distance, the squirrel muses. Steven blinks. He wonders if he's having a nervous breakdown.

You're not having a nervous breakdown,

the squirrel says.   Steven leans forward and stares. The squirrel does the same.

You'd be a very pretty girl,

the squirrel says to Steven.   Steven doesn't know how to respond.   The squirrel looks off to his left for a moment.

I am going to tell you some things and I need you to listen. I will not tell you your future or about the specifics of the future but I will reveal the future to you. The future as a concept. As an instance. This is not the best of all possible worlds. The world is not the world. We don't even realize what is possible. We sit in palaces of consumption and breed. I wonder if you will breed? Do you want children? I don't care. Don't have them. It's irresponsible to bring children into the world. It is a harsh, cruel place and no one will give a fuck about you or them except you and them. You are weak and you are stupid. Depend on no one except for yourself. Do not be beholden to anyone. This is the future. The future is not a hacienda which must be built. The hacienda has been burnt to the fucking ground. You lit the match. You did Steven. You are justified in hating yourself, in hating the idea of yourself. You're a fucking rapist and you haven't even touched a woman, have you? It's fine if you did. I once knew a boy, much like yourself, that confessed to me once that if he were really honest, he's never had consensual sex in his life. I asked what he meant and he said that the women he's slept with never said no, but they never said yes either. Did Natalie say yes Steven?

Steven starts to angry and his fists clench.

Fuck you, you weakling. What, you think because you kicked in the head of some Los Angeles wannabe porn star playboy faggot you can run roughshod over the rest of creation. I've met God. He's not fucking impressed.

Steven sighs, What the fuck is going on? and his shoulders slouch.

Good. Give in to it. Give into all that self pity. All of that loathing. You're broken, yes? Smashed to bits, yes? We know this. We've known it all along. We've been cleaved together like this. We have. You and I. Don't you recognize me? Don't you know me? Haven't you felt my presence? In the schoolyard. At the dinner table. You know me. You know my name. Say it.

Steven shakes his head.

I don't know you.

Say it.

I don't know you.

Say it.

I don't know you.

The squirrel stops and deliberately moves a bit closer.

When Kathy was 4 years old she was sitting in the play room of her parents. Kathy saw a doll sitting in the corner of the room that she had never seen before. The doll wore a powder blue dress with a red ribbon in her hair and blonde pigtails. Kathy thought the doll looked pretty. She shakily stood up and walked over to the doll and as she got closer she realized the doll was missing an eye. She bent over and looked closely at the doll's face. She wondered where the eye had gone. Kathy began crawling around on the floor frantically looking for the missing eye. She turns over her little plastic table, her plastic chairs, tears apart the pile of toys and stuffed animals, breathing heavily. She makes so much noise her mother comes in the room and finds Kathy crawling along the floor, her hands feeling along the hardwood. She asks Kathy, annoyed

What are you doing?

Kathy stops and looks up at her mother, tears running down her cheeks.

She can't see,

she says. When Kathy was 16 years old she went to a party in high school. The boys parents were away and six or seven of his friends were over and Kathy and two of her friends were there. They were drinking cheap beer and smoking dirt weed and listening to the boy's parents' record collection. The Carpenters were on. One of the boys says something about Karen Carpenter being anorexic, but not the hot kind. Kathy wonders if she is the hot kind. She hears two of the boys laughing in the other room. The other boys walk into the room to find out why. They start laughing as well. Two of the girls 44→
go outside to smoke but Kathy follows the boys. One of the boys sees Kathy walk into the room and says

Hey, I think we figured out what we're going to do later on tonight?

Okay, what?

Kathy says,

The boy who's house they are at says

Come over here and look.

He is sitting in front of a computer screen. As she walks

further into the room she hears what are clearly the sounds of people fucking. She walks around behind the boy and looks at the monitor. On it there are nine or ten men standing around another man jerking off while he fucks a young girl, 19 or 20. She sort of looks like me, Kathy thinks. All the boys laugh wildly as Kathy blankly stares at the screen. One of the boys shouts, What do you think? Care to volunteer? Kathy feels herself getting wet. She shakes her head as if to clear cobwebs, sneers and says,

I don't want to see this.

She storms out of the room into the bathroom and slams the door, listening to them laugh fitfully. She sits on the edge of the tub, listening to them laugh, shuts her eyes and imagines they are laughing at her as the boy who's house they are at fucks her doggystyle mercilessly while they stroke their cocks. She slips her hands down her pants and fingers herself furiously until she comes for a minute solid. Kathy is in Steven's apartment. She is thinking about that night when she was 16. Steven is fucking her face and Kathy has tears running down her face as she gags. She is fucking herself with a dildo that Steven had bought her earlier. She feels Steven's cock slipping out of her throat and she opens her eyes, her mascara streaking down her cheeks. She wishes the dildo inside of her were another man's cock. She wishes it was the boy who's house she was at's cock inside of her. She opens her eyes to see why Steven stopped fucking her mouth and just as she does he cums all over face and in her eyes. She flinches backwards and mutters,

45→ Ah, fuck,

as her eyes sting and she tears up even more. The salt of her tears and Steven's cum leaks down her cheeks, some collecting near the corner of her mouth and she almost instinctively uses her tongue to lick it up. Steven asks if she's okay. Kathy replies,

I can't see.

Steven and the other men drink cans of Mexican beer. Kathy doesn't drink any because she doesn't want her stomach to stick out. She sucks her stomach in and talks stupidly about how expensive New York is and pulls at her shorts. Kathy is wearing black jeans cut into shorts and her ass is hanging out. She is wearing a tight white tank top. Kathy has a good body. Steven and the other men tell Kathy that she has a good body. Kathy is anxious but also aroused and wonder if her anxiety is making blood rush to her cunt. Two men she doesn't know are touching her. One man is running his hands up and down the inside of her thigh and another man has his hand around the back of her neck. Her skin feels like it's on fire. Her cunt is wet and she feels betrayed by herself. The man running his hand up and down her thighs slips his fingers under her shorts and panties and tells the other men that Kathy is wet. There are eight or nine men, maybe ten. Two of them push Kathy onto the floor of the kitchen. Kathy think I do not want to dissociate and she doesn't dissociate. She feels every part of her body. A man with large calloused hands slips her tank top over her tits and examines her tits and flicks one of her nipples, hard. Another pulls her shorts and off and runs his hands over her ass cheeks. Another takes a wooden spoon from the counter and inserts its handle into her. She winces.

After this, you'll be able to fuck her with a baseball bat,

someone says. Kathy on her knees sucking one cock
then another then being fucked in the face by two and
literally feeling herself dripping onto the floor. Someone
pushing Kathy onto all fours and pushing a short thick
cock into her from behind while she sucks one cock and
then another and is then fucked in the face by two. The 46→
man fucking her drives three spitty fingers into her
asshole and fucks it.

Where should I cum?

the man asks.

Kathy,

Steven says. She looks up. He's been watching her suck cock. She can't respond because her mouth is full.

Beg him to cum inside you.

She can't beg because her mouth is full. The two men fucking her mouth stop fucking it.

Please,

she says.

Please what,

Steven says.

Please cum inside my cunt.

Keep saying it.

Please cum inside my cunt. Please cum inside my cunt. Please cum inside my cunt. Please cu

The man pushes his fingers deep into Kathy's ass and cums in her cunt. Steven sticks his fingers in her and puts some of the cum in her mouth and tells her to swallow it. Kathy's stomach feels empty. She feels like she's being stung everywhere by insects. She feels light. Steven feels like he and the other men in the room are one man. His movements are more violent than sexual. Kathy thinks her memory of this will be fuzzy because it is fuzzy. She wonders if the men feel this is a bonding experience. She thinks that a gangbang might be the most natural way to fuck. It's literally how human beings were designed to fuck each other. The shape of a cock made it sort of like a shovel. She is being fucked selfishly in the mouth and fucked selfishly in the ass and the selfishness makes her wetter. Each man cums inside of her ass or cunt or on her face at least once, and all but one, who is able to fuck many times in a row and keep cumming, start putting some of their clothes back on and drinking beer. Steven keeps his clothes off and watches the man who is still fucking Kathy fuck Kathy's cunt. Cum is dripping out of Kathy's cunt and ass and drying on her lips. She realizes that she felt sure that this would fuck her up but that she actually feels perfect. She cums finally as she feels the man cum in her a final time. She tightens her cunt, trying to pull as much cum as she can deep into her. She feels like it's filling her stomach and intestinal track, like it'll burst her organs and leak into her bloodstream. She screams.

You can't leave,

Steven says.

You have to stay here forever.

I can't,

Kathy says.

I live in New York.

You have to stay here now.

I like it better in New York. I live in New York now.

I'm going to come with you to New York then.

Steven holds Kathy and sniffs her hair.

Sometimes I get sad and then I get aroused, for what reasons I can't say,

Steven says.

I'm going to come to New York.

I'm here for another full week,

Kathy says.

You're going to get sick of me.

I love you,

Steven says.

You don't actually,

Kathy says.

Yes I do,

Steven says.

I love you so much and I'm coming with you to New York because I have to be with you all of the time. Or I'll just trap you in this room so you can never leave. I wish I could get you pregnant.

You're just saying things,

Kathy says.

Do you actually even feel connected to me? Do you ever just feel like the
49→ feeling you actually want is impossible so you try to create some semblance
of it? Like you're setting it up. It's scripted and everyone else has their own script, too, and no one has one that matches yours exactly.

You think I'm performing all the time,

Steven says.

I'm not performing. This isn't an act.

Kathy uses Steven's money to buy a first class ticket back to New York. She cries on the plane thinking she can never leave New York City again or she will die. She takes an Ativan and falls asleep on the plane next to a woman wearing a skirt suit. She takes a cab to her apartment and goes out to buy blonde hair dye and dyes her hair and goes to sleep.   Kathy feels rested in the morning. She puts ointment on the faint scars on her legs and brushes her teeth with an electric toothbrush. She checks her makeup on by the window to make sure it will look natural outside. She thinks about how feeling feminine makes her anxious. She puts on black tights and a long black sweater and short black boots. Kathy spends hundreds of dollars at Sephora and gets a rush from it. She is given several free samples of face cream.   Kathy nervously eats half of a bagel and has diarrhea in a bookstore bathroom. She goes to a department store and can't afford anything. Her hair needs to be toned. It's brassy. She is even thinner than before. She stops looking like a person and starts looking like a sick animal. Kathy calls a friend who she lived with in West Harlem when she was younger. The woman's name is Juana and she is prettier and bigger than Kathy. They meet at a shoe store on the Upper West Side. Juana tells Kathy that Kathy doesn't want to live in Harlem again, and that Kathy should sign up for a website that pairs women with good bodies with men with lots of money. Juana says the site is honest. Kathy agrees.   Juana makes Kathy buy a pair of pink heels and they go to Sephora. Juana puts makeup on Kathy. Kathy looks like a cartoon of a woman. They walk to the park and Juana takes photographs of Kathy wearing high heels and too much makeup on her cell phone. Juana sends the photos to Kathy's phone with a link to the website.

Alexina feels like stopping to sleep but Abel insists they keep walking. Alexina asks Abel where they are walking to. They had been hopping trains and crawling in the luggage compartments of buses—not much walking so much as frantic scurrying—but now it was just walking on sidewalks, climbing the occasional telephone pole and shimmying along wires. It was boring. Not exciting like darting up a ladder into a box car and hiding quietly in the rafters of the boxcar. Alexina asks Abel where they are. It tells her this place is called Newark. Alexina says it looks like a dump. Abel says it is. Alexina asks if Kathy is close by. Abel says she is across the river in Manhattan. Or at least that's where she was in the dream. Abel says that It wishes Walter Benjamin had lived long enough to see modern day Manhattan. Alexina asks who Walter Ben-jah-min is. Abel corrects her and says Ben-yah-mean. Alexina thinks that can't be right either. She doesn't tell Abel this. She doesn't care. She wants to ask Abel why It thinks this but she's sure It will end up telling her anyway so she says nothing. Abel's discourse never follows. Alexina tells Abel It must be depressed. Abel says It's just concentrating. Alexina asks Abel what there is to concentrate on. Abel says pheromones. Alexina nods slowly in silent comprehension. Abel is looking thin and winter is coming. Alexina is worried. Abel looks like the cats that normally stalk them. Alexina doesn't like the way Abel looks. She follows It. Then she sees Kathy walking out of the PATH station and lighting a cigarette. She taps Abel on the shoulder and points. Abel climbs a telephone pole and crawls
51→ along the wires across the street to Kathy. It crawls down the pole and scurries up to her. They are talking. Kathy looks scared. She backs away slowly from Abel and then stops. People are walking by Kathy and Abel, smiling and laughing, taking pictures with their phones. Kathy looks relaxed now. She is not talking. Alexina imagines Abel must be. Alexina knows how prone Abel is to running off at the mouth. As she sits beneath the bush across the street she feels around between her legs

trying to find her clitoris. She wonders what is taking Abel so long. She hears tires screech and Kathy shout out something and looks up and sees Abel darting in front of a car and stopping. The car runs over Abel and Alexina stares for a while. Then she sits down and tries to find her clitoris again. Gradually Alexina stops thinking. She stops hearing words. She stops feeling for her clitoris. She paws at something in the dirt. She picks it up and chews it. She drops it and suddenly her head darts up into the bushes. She looks left and then right. She climbs into and through the bush and over to an old oak tree. She hears a dog bark and climbs the tree. She does not look back at Abel. She does not cry. She does not see Kathy crying. She does not feel sad. She doesn't remember Abel. Or Kathy. Or what a clitoris is. Kathy looks up from Abel's crushed body and sees Alexina sitting in the branch of the tree. Alexina looks completely devoid of thought, emotion, and expression. She sits on the branch and occasionally picks at some bark or scampers up or down the branch then comes back to the same spot and sits staring through the leaves. Kathy wishes she could be like Alexina. Kathy wishes she could be like Abel. Kathy texts Steven. The text says he is dead. She waits; Steven responds and asks who is dead. Kathy says the squirrel is dead. Steven does not answer. It is the last thing Kathy ever texts to Steven.

The blackened tooth in the old bum's mouth. Something bruised and something borrowed he remembered her saying once. Terror or something like it kisses him softly on the forehead. Lights a cigarette. This is all happening in his head, in Steven's head. Stares a while longer at the bum. How did she know I know he's wondering. Should I tell him now I wonder. Paris was her least favorite city but he always was a Francophone. He wishes he could be like Querelle—cold, manipulative, feral, criminal. Little does he know that, in fact, he plays the role well. He looks at Kathy's text again. The squirrel. Steven shuts his eyes and tries to imagine Kathy staring at this flattened squirrel carcass. Then he thinks of Querelle again. He thinks of when Genet writes, She was happy, and perfectly in line with the tradition of those women they used to call 'ruined', 'fallen', feckless bitches in heat, ravished dolls, sweet sluts, instant princesses, hot numbers, great lays, succulent morsels, everybody's darlings... Steven thought about Kathy and smiled slowly. It comforted him. He cared more about Abel (even though he didn't know that was his name) then he did about Kathy. He tried to remember how he knew the Genet quote. He'd read the first ten pages of the book before he lent it to someone and never got it back. He saw the Fassbinder film. He went on Goodreads and noticed the quote immediately. All of my erudition comes from the Internet, Steven thinks. Steven gets up and walks to the cabinet. He takes out a rocks glass and pours himself a short pour of scotch. He thinks it is so typical of him to dramatize the perverted coupling of shock and boredom. Steven remembers when
53→ the squirrel approached him after he nearly killed the man in his parents house. He remembered everything the squirrel told him that day. About Kathy. How he would meet her. How he would forever be a ruiner. A deceiver. How he would hate himself and not be able to help himself. How he would be more charming than he had a right to be. He remembered smiling as he heard the squirrel tell him all of this. He knew it was true. It was true now. Guilt without remorse is penance without

action. Steven feels dizzy. A moth flutters against the light in the kitchen. Piles of dead wings. Thick lipstick layers on a napkin. Steven sinks to the floor. His head feels like it is caving in. He knows I am there.

He cannot see me but he knows. It's something like crying. Something like missing someone. No tears come. Promise me that you won't ever forget your own wolf-like nature. That you will never separate sinew from bone and taste the warm, stinking marrow oozing onto your soft pallet and rationalize it. That you will not aestheticize it as I have done. When there is nothing left to consume, no more want, we will consume what we love. And what we hate. We bring it in and we push it out. Consumption and excretion. There is a dream of America. It is not the American dream. You know it's name. I know what you're thinking. Trying to explain it. Trying to aestheticize it. The terror. The delusion. You are the feckless bitch in heat. I doubt you are a good lay. An instant princess. And insistent princess. Squinting. It's the next to last quote on Goodreads you are trying to remember. Here you are having a nervous breakdown trying to demonstrate your erudition to a dead fucking squirrel broken and scooped into dumpster by a Dunkin Donuts on the other side of the country. The rims of his eyelids were burning. A blow received straightens a man up and makes the body move forward, to return that blow, or a punch—to jump, to get a hard-on, to dance: to be alive. Do you have a hard on Steven? You fucking faggot. Are you hard you pathetic... You are I can tell. A prophet if ever there were one. The visitation is nigh. Hoping it would be more like that scene in *Angels in America*: the ceiling caving in. The sexless herald straddling you. It's not. It's a fist, elbow deep in your ass. A hand wrapping around your prostate and squeezing it. The first rush of nausea. The spurt of infected cum and piss staining the front of your trousers. Doubling over in masochistic ecstasy. For the first time. But a blow received may also cause you to bend over, to shake, to fall down, to die. When we see life, we call it beautiful. When we see death, we call it ugly. But it is more beautiful still to see oneself living at great speed, right up to the moment of death. Something about the French and the transubstantiation of the ugly and depraved into beauty. Daniel, Rabelais, Voltaire, Balzac, Flaubert, Lautreamont, Baudelaire, Rimbaud, Lorrain and Genet. The beauty of hating beauty. The beauty of negation. Of destruction. Of abjection. I suppose the Anglophiles have their equivalent. And the Russians. Even your generation. An entire mass of people dedicated to the power and beauty of irony. It is beautiful to you all. The sad nostalgia for a past never shared and experience never had. Satirizing the late adolescent and early adulthood equivalent of dress-up but at middle age. The stunted growth. Impotent. Infected by a ceaseless desire for self-forgetting. For fashion. For fashionable irony. To offend those incapable of being offended. The enlightened sarcoma on the shoulder of this whore, the United States of America. This cancer is self-aware and determined to spread without killing the host. Anorexic coke habits sucking at the teat of a trust fund for fucking nourishment. There are no people just ciphers. Groping and clawing. Consensual non-consent bleeding like cheap laundry detergent in fine sheets until consent is impossible to give or receive. Everything is taken with a soft, thick-wristed hand wrenching out of it's socket. The detectives, poets, domestic servants and priests all rely on abjection. From it, they draw their power. It circulates in their veins. It nourishes them. You hate them and are one of them. Stand up. Try to anyway.

Steven tries and collapses back onto the floor, a thin milky white gelatinous ooze seeping from his rectum. Finally Steven starts crying. He tries to smile but his face is frozen in a mask of incredulous horror. Steven thinks about Kathy standing in the street staring at the dead squirrel. He imagines her getting hit by a speeding taxi. He imagines coming across her in the street and violating her near-corpse. Fucking the wounds from her compound fractures. Re-arranging her organs to create bile and blood lubricated sheaths in which to bury his cock. He shuts his eyes hard and tries to scream but only a long strand of spittle escapes from between his teeth. He wishes he could throw up. Steven keeps crying and keeps trying to smile. Steven imagines Kathy's funeral. Her despondent parents. Her ex-boyfriends. He imagines them all toasting to her memory at the well attended and opulent wake. He imagines standing in the back of the room at her wake laughing quietly to himself. He falls asleep shuddering, dark circles under his eyes, in a pool of his own piss and cum. He thinks he might be dying. He hopes they find him soon, just like this—tears fresh on his cheeks and his mouth twisted into the inexplicable smile of an ecstatic saint at the moment of their martyrdom.

You should call it the broad and ceaseless mythology of desperation. You are the statue that speaks. Your eyes comprise ten percent of your head. It is not your mouth that speaks. The mask of the idol speaks in my mind and you are it's voice. I will dress you in robes and garlands. Appease you. Wash your mouth out with holy water and sweet herbs. Speak. I pray to you to speak now in my dreaming. Give voice to my other voice. Are you angry? Playful? Say unto the Gardener that a cursed one will not be able to stand before him. The polished surface of its side his hearing makes known; its writing which is engraved his hearing makes known; the light of the torch assists his hearing. Appeasing the liver. Counsellor, exceeding wise commander, princess of all the great gods, exalted speaker, whose utterance is unrivaled. I have taken note of the portents. Let me rest now. Let me sleep. I'm still sleeping mom. He's still sleeping. Let her rest. Let us sleep.

Kathy found herself on her computer in the library looking at drawings by Vesalius. She wasn't quite sure how she stumbled upon them or what occasioned her to look at them. She thought they were beautiful. Seemingly sexless bodies skinned and frozen in motion. Muscle, fascia, tendon and joint. Connective tissue. Their faces always seemed as if they were in the most calm and yet most painful state possible. She imagined these figures, always set in some grotto or courtyard, a small archway or shrine or cluster of buildings in the background, wandering through the Low Countries. Speechless. She imagined it would hurt too much to flex the necessary muscles to enunciate. Instead just tongueless, toothless verbiage. If one could call it that. Incantatory gibberish. Would they ask for help? Would they search out other bodies to cling to, to commingle the sticky residue of blood and fat to their absconded shell, their unlimbered sheaths, clinging stubbornly to the bodies of these Others. Kathy wondered what she would do were she one of these living anatomical illustrations. These strange compendiums of scientific curiosity and the humanist capacity for the grotesque and macabre. She thought of Dante's depiction of hell. And Bosch. And Goya. How the Renaissance and the early eras of humanism produced such enlightenment coupled with such horror. As if the Dark Ages, those Olde English poems of Norse invasions and Celtic ape creatures wondering the marshlands, the town squares of doctors in those ever-so-fashionable with steampunk and fantasy metal fans plague masks had become so fully integrated into humanity's collective unconscious that even in the midst of scientific and medical advancement and staggering growth in commerce and communication there was a specter haunting rationality. The sleep of Reason...which produces monsters. Kathy thought about the museum of death in Los Angeles, nestled in some bungalow just down the street from the Walk of Fame, right off Sunset. They had a piece of the cabinet that Rozz Williams hung himself from. Serial killer art. A detailed collection of material surrounding Ed Gein.

The ur-serial killer. And of course Manson. The Black Dahlia. Not much about Zodiac though. She thought of San Francisco and she thought of Steven. She thought that Steven might be able to kill someone but that he wouldn't. The switch wasn't quite all the way flipped, Kathy muttered to herself. She wondered why that phrase seemed to stealthily find its way to her lips. Why she felt the need to give voice to that thought. She wondered if deep down in the pit of her stomach she didn't feel some faint bit of hope. If she had some reason to believe that everything would be alright. She looked up from the computer and saw a homeless man sitting in the corner with a copy of New York Review of Books covering his lap, staring at her wide eyed, his hand furiously pumping his cock. She took a sip of her coffee and logged onto her Fetlife account on her phone and looked up the New York Review of Books website on Google. She clicked and scanned the table of contents. She wondered which article the homeless man would end up coming on. Kathy got wet. She hoped it was the Zadie Smith essay.

Kathy meets Marc in a bar near his office.

She is wearing her most expensive dress and her new high heels and her eyes are big like a child's. Marc works in marketing. He is only a few years older than Kathy but has made a lot of money. His parents were not rich but he is rich. He isn't particularly good looking, but has a new haircut and a suit that fits him well and fashionable glasses. He isn't ugly; he just doesn't look like anything.

You're just my type,

Marc says. He puts his hands around her waist to see if they're big enough to fit around it. He buys her a vodka tonic without asking her what she drinks. She drinks the vodka tonic. She is wearing new underwear. He slides his hand up her thigh. She looks at him and tries to communicate that she isn't sure what to do.

What type of arrangement are we getting into here,

Marc says.

I like you. You're just my type.

I don't have any money,

Kathy says.

You're an artist,

Marc says.

Sure,

Kathy says.

You need somewhere to live,

Marc says.

You want to go shopping. You want to get haircuts and go to a nicer gym.

I don't go to the gym,

Kathy says.

Will you fuck me,

59→

Marc says.

Will you fuck me and call me Daddy when you fuck me and call me Daddy whenever we're together and no one can hear you.

Yeah,

Kathy says.

I mean, I like that. I've done that before.

I don't want to hear about what you've done before,

Marc says.

Okay, Daddy,

Kathy says.

I'd like to give you some money now,

Marc says.

I will give you the same amount every week if you're a good girl. Maybe someday I will give you more. Maybe someday you'll move in with me and you can have whatever you want. I will give you everything. You might think I'm boring. I'm sure you think I'm boring. I go to therapy. I'm a troubled person. I'm sure we'll get along. You're just my type.

Marc gives Kathy an envelope filled with hundred dollar bills. It is the most money Kathy has ever held in her hand. She puts it in her purse and considers leaving and getting a cab but she doesn't want to leave.

Thanks, Daddy,

she says.

I love you very much, baby,

Marc says.

You just met me,

Kathy says.

It's part of the role play,

Marc says.

Oh,

Kathy says.

That's fine then.

Will you say it back,

Marc says.

Sure,

Kathy says.

Say it,

Marc says.

I love you, Daddy,

Kathy says.

Good girl,

Marc says.

Let me show you where Daddy lives.

They take a cab to Marc's apartment in the Village. His

furniture is modern and arranged thoughtfully. He has lots of books and magazines. Things are tidy. Kathy sits on his couch and hikes her skirt up so her legs show.

Baby,

Marc says.

You have to stop doing things like that. You know what it does to Daddy. And we can't. It's wrong.

You don't like me,

Kathy says.

Of course I like you,

Marc says.

Do you like me like me,

Kathy says.

What do you mean?

Like the way a boyfriend and girlfriend like each other.

Baby, I'm not sure what you mean.

I know you do, Daddy. You look at me like the boys at school do. The ones who have crushes on me.

I hate thinking about those boys. I do like you, but it isn't right.

None of those boys make me feel funny like you do.

Funny?

Marc sits down next to Kathy and pulls her onto his lap.

Yeah,

Kathy says.

Like when I get in bed next to you. Or when I sit on your lap, like now.

She turns around so she's facing him and wraps her legs around him.

I don't understand what it means, really, but I feel funny,

61→ she says.

What does it feel like?

I feel achy between my legs. I start breathing faster and I feel hot.

Daddies have a part that gets achy, too.

I know about that from health class,

Kathy says. She is wet and grinding her cunt against Marc. He is hard.

What did they teach you?

Daddy.

I'm going to cum.

What's that?

You'll feel it in just a second.

I feel something shooting in me, Daddy.

Marc cums inside of her. She stands up and rubs some cum off of her thigh.

It's dripping out of me,

she says.

Taste it,

he says. She puts her fingers in her mouth. He gets up and goes to the bathroom. He runs the faucet. Kathy picks up a design magazine and flips through it. She wants to go to sleep.

Will you stay over,

Marc calls from the bathroom.

What,

Kathy says. Marc comes back from the bathroom and sits in a chair across from Kathy.

That was heavy, wasn't it.

I don't think so.

I want to do this all the time. I want you to stay. Do you have an apartment?

Sort of,

Kathy says.

I can stay here. It's not a big deal. It's just a power exchange thing. You don't need to be upset.

Thank you. You're so nice to me. Can we watch teevee together? Do you like to watch teevee? I bet you aren't interested in teevee?

63→ I love teevee,

Kathy says.

We can watch as much teevee as you want.

Are you hungry?

No.

I'll order some Thai food. Do you eat meat?

Sure.

I really like you, and I hope you like me.

I do like you,

Kathy says.

I think you're sweet. I'm sorry you got anxious. It's okay.

You're so good to Daddy,

Marc says, and turns on the television.

64→

It always reminded her of other summers. It wasn't all that long ago that her mother reminded her of that vacation. It always seemed like some distant memory. It was five years ago. She remembered masturbating in the shower behind their beach house, biting down hard on a wash cloth. The lukewarm outdoor shower water raining down on her head. But those were other summers; summers when it was still possible to approach her own body with a sense of wonder. When she could see herself as a mother. When her mother died her father never cried. He never really did much of anything. She wasn't a person to any man she ever knew, not even to him. She was his little girl, but that's not the same thing as being a person. She always wanted to be more than what she was. Don't get the wrong impression—she didn't feel as if she were incomplete or broken, not even a little. She was not damaged because of some deep trauma or some crushing neglect. It was the sort of damage that occurs in shipping or production. Functional incompatibly. It was just the way she liked it. She could be a dream that crossed the sky. There's a tomorrow somewhere in there, she thinks, remembering the lyrics to the song on that old shower radio the first time she remembered thinking that her mother was going to die someday. It's hard to dance when you can't swallow. It was easy to imagine a world without him. Mother, the car is here. The church bells brought her right back to that distant summer, that distant summer of new shorelines and littered beaches. She missed the sound of the gulls and the wind rushing through the grass in the dunes. You
65→ could hear them dancing in the parking lot while she smoked a cigarette, staring at the hearse. I want to be a real boy, she thought. It was her favorite movie as a child. Now it's all lost in the dissonance.

Marc enjoyed listening to jazz in college. Marc had sophisticated taste in jazz. At least that's what his music appreciation professor told him. Marc's taste for jazz didn't emerge from any sort of substantial or emotional place. It just helped him project an image he found useful. Marc liked spending money even when he didn't have it. He used the credit card his father gave him liberally. Marc didn't care. His father didn't care either. Marc originally studied finance. Macro-economics. In his sophomore year he changed his major to marketing. By his junior year Mark had a good internship. All of the other juniors in the marketing department were jealous. Marc had his own apartment off campus. Marc always had girls over. Freshmen mostly. Marc enjoyed sleeping with as many of them as possible during the week and trying to guess how many of them were virgins based purely on the sex. He never asked. He never cared. Sex was more about deploying power. It was about claiming some part of himself that allowed him to feel as if he were in control. After he sent whatever girl he had in his apartment home, they would never stay the night, that is when Marc would get to work. Projects, proposals, busy work. It was inspiring to feel dominion over another person's emotions and sensation. Marc graduated in 2003. He went on to get an MBA. He completed that program and graduated in 2006. He immediately got an interview with a large and well-regarded firm. Marc bought a new suit for the interview. On his way to the interview he stopped and bought a cappuccino. He sat in the lobby and sipped it carefully. He shuffled some magazines around on the end table. He loved this lobby.
66→
He loved the furniture. The marble floors. The art deco fixtures. The secretary called Marc's name. Marc threw away his remaining cappuccino and followed the secretary. She was tall and had great legs and a slender waist. Her dress was emerald green and she wore a thick black belt with a modest gold buckle, black stockings, and modest black heels. Marc stared at her ass as he followed her and then noticed her slowing

down and looked at some of the pictures on the wall. Art from campaigns the firm had worked on. His face registered nothing, no sense of nervousness, no sense of intimidation.He wanted to appear unflappable. He walked into the office and shook hands with the man behind the desk. The man behind the desk didn't introduce himself. He wore a black suit, white French cuff dress shirt with white gold cufflinks, solid red tie, a tie-bar which matched his cufflinks with an engraved filagree. His hair was salt and pepper and parted to the right. It was thinning ever so slightly. University of Chicago undergrad, Columbia MBA.

Interview anywhere else yet?

the man asked.

No,

Marc replied. The man gestured at a chair and Marc sat down. The man offered Marc water or coffee. Marc asked for a club soda with a wedge of lemon. The man buzzed the intercom and told the secretary what Marc wanted. The man asked Marc what he thought of some marketing campaign the company had just launched. Marc immediately began conversing in a way both natural and yet clearly prepared, in the scholastic sense. He knew exactly how to control an interview. Be at ease, but be informed. Demonstrate that you are in the know, but don't seem desperate to give the right answer. For him it was in a way no different then picking up a woman. So where are you from? can be a one word answer or it can be an entr'acte into your life. You just had to read the person asking the question. Marc could read the
67→ man behind the desk. The secretary interrupted with a knock. She opened the door without waiting for an answer and handed Marc his drink. He said thank you. She nodded and left.

Married?

the man asked Marc.

No,

Marc responded.

Girlfriend?

No.

Boyfriend?

I'm not gay.

I don't care.

The man paused for a moment. He spoke up again.

You want to get married?

I dunno.

Don't.

Marc arched an eyebrow a bit.

When's the last time you get laid?

Excuse me,

Marc asks. Not taken aback. Just a matter of fact way of asking Did I hear you right? without seeming antagonistic.

When's the last time you got laid?

Marc answered immediately,

Last night.

No girlfriend?

No.

The man behind the desk smirked a bit.

You're hired.

68→

Marc Wright

Lives in: New York, New York

Birthday: February 3, 1981

Relationship Status: This field left private

Where he works: S/FB Marketing & Consulting, Inc.

[Click on About]

Work and Education:

Graduate School

Columbia University | Class of 2006 | Masters of Business Administration | Marketing / Corporate Branding & Social Media / Demographics | New York City, New York

College

University of Chicago | Class of 2003 | Marketing & Finance | Minor in Japanese | Chicago, Illinois

Job

Project Director, Vice-President of Marketing & Research Strategy | S/FB Marketing & Consulting, Inc.

Living

New York City, New York (Current City) | Chicago, Illinois (Hometown)

69→

History By Year

2010: Promoted to Vice President of Marketing & Research Strategy at S/FB Marketing & Consulting, Inc.

2009: Named Project Director at S/FB Marketing & Consulting, Inc.

2007: Hired at S/FB Marketing & Consulting, Inc.

2006: Graduated from Columbia University

2003: Graduated from University of Chicago

1981: Born on February 3

About Marc

I am currently Vice President of Marketing & Research Strategy at S/FB Marketing & Consulting. I enjoy post-World War II Japanese literature, art, and design. Something of an amateur tech junkie. I enjoy traveling to Japan a couple of times a year both for business and leisure. Maintain and curate a blog on cultural and aesthetic trends in Japan for both professionals and people in the creative arts. Inbox me if you would like more information.

70→

Basic Info

Birthday: February 3, 1981

Sex: Male

Languages: English, Japanese, French, German

Religious Views: Atheist

Political Views: Moderately agnostic

Contact Info

Address: New York City, New York

Screenames: mwright_sfb (Skype)

Website: http://www.sfb.org |

http://www.mangeiblog.com

Email: marc.wright@sfb.org

Networks: University of Chicago, Columbia University, S/FB, American Marketing Association, Bloom Japan, Japan Brand

Favorite Quotations

True beauty is something that attacks, overpowers, robs, and finally destroys. —Yukio Mishima

Of all the kinds of decay in this world, decadent purity is the most malignant. —Yukio Mishima

What is fetish, what is stylization, and what is simple specificity? —William T. Vollman

71→

Pages Liked

S/FB Marketing & Consulting, Inc.; Mangei Blog; American Marketing Association; Bloom Japan; Japan Brand; William Gibson; William T. Vollman; Yukio Mishima; Haruki Murakami; Kobo Abe; Sawako Nakayasu; Noh Theater; Phillip Roth; Ernest Hemingway; Constructivism; Shiego Fukuda; Akira Kurosawa; Mikio Naruse; Ishiro Honda; Yasujiro Ozu; Hayao Miyazaki; Takeshi Kitano; Jean Luc Godard; Woody Allen; Lars von Trier; Paul Thomas Anderson; Michael Haeneke; David O. Russell; Wes Anderson; Noah Baumbach; Martin Scorsese; Film Noir; Orson Welles; Alfred Hitchcook; Fritz Lang; Wim Wenders; Werner Herzog; Errol Morris; Alexander Rodchenko; El Lissitzky; Herbet Bayer; Paul Schuitema; Miles Davis; Joe Henderson; Dave Holland; Bill Evans; Billy Taylor; Chicago Blackhawks; Chicago White Sox; Jean Luc-Godard; Toru Takemitsu; Kurt Schwitters; Sidney Bechet; Bix Biederbecke; Sarah Vaughn; Joe Lovano; John Scofield; Pat Metheny; Johannes Brahms; Claude Debussy; Oliver Messiaen; Tolouse-Lautrec; Paul Verlaine; Arthur Rimbaud; John Cage; Jean Sibelius; Led Zeppelin; The Rolling Stones; The Strokes; Lou Reed; The Velvet Underground; The Doors; John Coltrane; Ornette Coleman; Archie Shepp; Andy Warhol; Robert Rauschenberg; Roy Lichtenstein; MoMA New York; Museo Guggenheim Bilbao; Solomon R. Guggenheim Museum; National Museum of Art, Kyoto; Mori Art Museum; Peggy Guggenheim Collection; design-dautore.com; Can Do Design; American Demographics; View Point; Journal of Marketing; Marketing Research; Communication Arts; Print Magazine; Pitchfork; Hans Fallada; Nick Tosches; Henri-Cartier Bresson; Yo La Tengo; Shugo Tokumaru; The Weekend; LCD Soundsystem; Brad Mehldau; Keith Jarrett; Paul Bley;

72→

Addenda

Marc Wright has 515 Friends.

Marc Wright has 126 photos. He is tagged and appears in 34 of them.

He has checked in to over 1,000 places on his map and the check-ins range from restaurants, bars, stores, museums and other venues all across cities like New York, Bilbao, Boston, Philadelphia, San Francisco, Seattle, Atlanta, Austin, Tokyo, Kyoto, Osaka, Chiba, Nagano, Kanagawa, Bangkok, Beijing, Moscow, Antwerp, Copenhagen, London, Leeds, Dublin, Edinburgh, Paris, Lyons, Marseilles, Venice, Rome, Dusseldorf, Berlin, Munich, Geneva, Prague, Budapest, and Zagreb.

Marc Wright does not have a Tumblr (at least not one he advertises on Facebook), but he aimlessly searches through it often.

His Twitter is connected to his Facebook and largely consists of re-tweeting pictures, articles, and links from various professional contacts or posts related to his blog or Tweets he finds worthy of sharing made by people more famous than he is. These occur only frequently enough to justify continuing to follow him (2-4 times a week).

73→

Kathy buying everything Helmut Lang at Barneys and feeling sort of smug and knowing she feels smug and feeling smug about her smugness. Kathy always had a good body and now she has a good skincare regimine. Kathy wearing baggy black asymmetrical anything with tights. Not getting high, drinking only top shelf, going to the best gym, staying hydrated, taking anti-depressants. Developing a new level or maybe depth of anxiety. Living in someone else's apartment, not working, reading magazines.

Thinking I'm an adult now and this is a job. Blaming her mother for not being a strong female role model. More shopping. Thinking about starting a fashion blog but never following through. Thinking yeah, I guess I came here imagining some bohemian whatever, but this is better. Thinking about methods of closet organization. Thinking I make jokes about how shallow and vain I am so everyone knows that I know, then thinking ha ha ha. Thinking all of the weakness that others perceive in me is barely weaknesses because I know about it. At least I'm self-aware. I would even know if I lost myself. These pills don't make me feel any different. I know I don't see my body the way other people see it, but I still feel a vague sense of superiority because I know intellectually that I'm not fat. I hate New York. How could anyone live anywhere else. I feel disconnected. Don't think empty. I don't feel empty. I just feel full of the wrong things.

Kathy knowing that her social media makes her look very, very happy, and thinner than she is, and prettier than she is, and like she has lots of money.

I wanted to be a civil rights leader. I wanted to preach non-violence. I wanted to work with youth. I'm the worst kind 74→
of whore because no one has a problem with this kind of prostitution. And, for fuck's sake, shame on anyone who thinks I was ruined by sex, or by sexual violence, or that I'm ruined at all. A person can't be ruined, or everything's ruined from the start and that's no fault of mine.

It isn't like Kathy hasn't gone to therapy and gotten the same old answers. Try to be alone, see what it's like to be alone, get to know yourself.

I know myself too well, Kathy knows. Consciousness is a punishment for something I'm sure I didn't do. I don't know anyone whose life isn't an attempt to forget itself. Of course there are things worth fighting for. Human progress is real. Things are better for my fag and dyke friends. My fag and dyke friends can get married and that's really important. No more stop and frisk. People deserve to be treated with some sort of dignity and I have my damn priorities straight. I told my therapist that I was afraid of death, yeah, and she told me it was a state change, like falling asleep, and asked if I was afraid of falling asleep. I was after she said that. I became aware of the state change. I started watching television that year. I love television. I want to be on television. I sometimes think of everything I do as being on television. I think that's how most people think. That's sort of what it looks like to be a person, from the inside. I know nothing is wrong with me. I understand what my upbringing resulted and didn't result in and I was as damaged or undamaged by
75→ my parents as anyone. I refuse super basic cause and effect, false causality, things are more complicated. It's so tempting to reduce. If I do anything, I want to not be reductive. And fuck anyone who doesn't realize I'm paying attention, or don't fuck them, because I don't think they know what they're looking for, and I need to remember, shit, how little anyone else is really thinking about me at all.

It wasn't long before the water started rising. She was lost, she was missing herself. She saw herself on a wanted poster covered in dead leaves. It was all new to her. He was always new to her. She believes that when she wades into the river it will fill her. It will flush out her insides. It will flush out him with him. She knows the current like the inside of a wound. He knows the wound like the current of the river. He can't ever understand it. It's always changing. The beauty makes his ears ring. He can't hear her now. She doesn't know what to say anyway. It's raining hard. He's harder than the rain. He found it for her and took it for himself. Now he knows what she knows. The pain frees them from the current. Eventually the pain finds them both. Eventually the water takes them both. It's always changing. They're always changing. Oh how they come and go...

You have taken me on many walks like this before. You have brought me along for all of these. You want the company so you don't feel alone, don't feel pathetic. You are always alone unless you are with me. You are always with me. You are watching a man and a woman sit at a set of metal chairs and a metal table on the sidewalk in front of a café on the Upper West Side. You are sitting on a bench facing away from the park. You have been watching them sit there and sip their drinks and eat their food for fifteen or twenty minutes maybe. You finally work up the courage. You get up to walk over and gently tug on my lead. You briefly look behind you to see if I am following. You smile when you see that I am. You cross the street briskly and walk over the seating area of the sidewalk café. You run your hand along the brass railing separating the seating area from the pedestrian part of the sidewalk. You walk up to the podium at the entrance of the seating area and tell the hostess you need a table for two and the hostess laughs. You smile a bit at the hostess and while she bites her lip and blushes you ignore her and look out of the corner of your eye to see if the man and woman you have been watching are laughing too. You notice that they are not; you notice they are talking. You notice that they do not notice you. Your face grows a bit sullen. After you are seated you ask the hostess if I can have some water. You nod at her when she smiles again and says,

Sure! It's a hot day out, isn't it cutie?

You look down at me and nod. You have been seated at a table at which your chair is directly behind the man's. You can't believe your good fortune. You are back to back with him. You can hear every word of their conversation. You thank the hostess when she comes back with my water and puts it in front of me. You look down and watch me drink a little and then lay down with my head under the shade of your table. You smile a bit. When you look up at the hostess she asks you what you would like to drink. You order a large Americano in a to-go cup, no room for cream, and a salted caramel bar. You thank the hostess again when she tells you that she'll be right back with your order. You cannot believe your good fortune as you notice there's been a lull in the man and woman's conversation the entire time you've been ordering. As you settle in to your seat you pull the paperback from your back pocket and open it to the page with the bookmark. You pretend to be reading but you stare at the same page with a mechanical pencil in your hand. Every so often you scribble something in the margins. You do this so that the people sitting around you will think you are engrossed in your book. You are not. You try to block out all distractions, even me. You double check to make sure the loop of my lead is wrapped around the sturdy leg of your chair. You are satisfied that it is secure. You listen.

77→

Do you want to go to that party later?

You wonder what party he could be referring to.

How crowded do you think it will be?

You find her voice pleasant, if a bit raspy. You write in the margin of you paperback: She smokes. Or is ill.

I doubt that it will be too crazy. Melanie and John's apartment isn't that big really. He's still a relative newcomer to the firm.

You write in the margin of your paperback: He must be somewhat well-to-do.

Oh, okay. I suppose we can stop by for a minute then. What time would we have to get there?

I dunno. 10pm?

Earlier. 9.

What's the point in even going then? No one will be there but us. We might as well just stay in tonight and just go out to dinner with them some other time.

Will they be angry?

No. John is hardly more than an acquaintance. I bet the only reason he invited me is because I'm his boss and he wants to kiss ass.

Oh, okay. Then yeah, let's not go.

Sounds good to me.

And a tall Americano and salted caramel bar for you.

Your gaze shoots up from your book and you see the hostess sliding your order onto the table.

I'm sorry! I startled you.

78→

You tell her it's fine. Really, don't worry, you say. You wave her off as she apologizes again and you tell her you're fine, that you were just lost in thought. You take the lid off of your Americano and blow on it a bit and take a sip. You think it's decent espresso. You write in your paperback that you should stop here again for coffee. You take a bite of your salted caramel bar. You think it's stale and too sweet. You put it down on the plate and you will not touch it for the rest of the time we are at the café. You tell the hostess everything is fine when she walks over to ask you how everything is. You lie to her. You follow her as she walks over to the man and the woman's table behind you. You listen intently as she tells them here is your check. You notice only he says thank you. You hear someone light a cigarette. You notice it takes a bit longer than it should if the person smoking were sitting directly behind you. You write:

Ha! I was right!

next to where you wrote that she smokes in your paperback. You look down at me because I've stirred. You stroke my back as I take a few more sips of the water and circle and lay down again. You hold your breath for a moment as the man accidentally elbows the arm of your chair as he reaches for his wallet.

Oh, I'm sorry

you hear him say. You don't even turn to look at him. You hurriedly reply,

That's fine. That's fine.

You hear a chair being pushed out and you hear someone walking behind you and then out of your peripheral vision you see her walk next to your table and squat and pet me. He's
79→ so sweet and handsome you hear her say. You look down at me and say,

Yes, he is.

You tell her I am six years old when she asks how old I am. You look at me looking into her face, mouth open, tongue hanging out slightly, ears perked up a bit. You tell her I am a yellow lab when she asks what breed I am. You hear the man clear his throat and watch her stand up. You chuckle a bit as she says,

Nice to meet you, sweet boy,

as she stands up. You wave goodbye and say nothing as she says,

Thanks for letting me pet him,

as they walk out of the seated area. Your eyes follow them as they walk towards the northwest corner of the intersection, maybe a third of a mile down the sidewalk, before you hurriedly stand up. You apologize to me as I jump up and whip my head around, wondering what the hell is going on. You throw $10 onto the table and pick up the small, empty water glass on the table and slip it into the bag from the tote bag bookstore you have been carrying. You pick up your Americano and hurriedly walk out of the seating area. The hostess calls,

Have a nice day,

after you and you ignore her, head forward posture, walking to the northwest corner of the intersection. You walk slowly to the corner and as the light changes you quicken your pace a bit to get within ear shot. You think that you are lucky it is a quiet Sunday afternoon. You crane your neck a bit, fifteen or twenty steps beside them and can hear most of what they say.

Marc, I forgot to tell you I might need some money for tomorrow.

What for?

I need some things. From the store. For around the house and other things.

Could you be more vague, Kathy?

You smile when he turns and you can see his profile and
notice he's smirking a bit at her. She doesn't seem to respond 80→
and you furrow your brow. You aren't sure what's going on
here. You follow behind them, trying not to breathe too
loudly, nor step too forcefully. The last thing you want to
do is draw attention to yourself.

Did you do your chores?

you hear him say.

Yes, I did all my chores.

You look down at me as if to see if I have registered all of this. You shake your head as I look up at you for a moment and then look ahead again, sniffing the trees planted in the dirt squares in the sidewalk.

That's my good girl, you hear him say.

I like it when you tell me I'm a good girl.

I bet you do. You always get such nice treats for being a good girl.

You actually stop for a moment and catch a gasp in your throat as you hear her say,

It makes me all achy down there again whenever you say it, daddy.

You can't believe what you are hearing. You take out the paperback, dropping the coffee into a trashcan and scribble frantically into the book. You are taking notes on the conversation, not editorializing. You think it's pretty obvious what's going on here. You cannot believe your good fortune. You are well out of earshot and see them chatting with the doorman at a building that you went to a party at once. You used to have one sort-of friend, an A&R guy for some label, at your old job at the record store. You remember he used to come in looking for rare Jamaican ska, dub, and soul 45s and the occasional rock or pop record. When you took the job at the bookstore though, you never bothered to keep in touch. As soon as they turned and walked inside you sauntered over to the entrance and tried to walk in casually.

Excuse me, sir,

you hear the doorman say. You stop and reply,

Oh, I'm here to see my friend, Terrence Jaynes.

You chuckle as the doorman tells you he's sure that's fine,
but he wanted to ask you how old I was. You tell him I just
81→ recently turned six and he leans down and pats me on the
head. You shake your head and wave off the doorman when
he asks if you'd like him to ring Mr. Jaynes and tell him
that you are an old friend and wanted to surprise him. You
smile as the doorman says that's fine and tells you to have
a nice day. You bound up the stairs looking left and right
in the foyer for an elevator or something and don't see one.
You walk past an unmanned desk and see a hallway to your
right. You look down it and see Marc and Kathy and Marc

unlocking the door and hear Kathy laugh softly. They go inside. You take out the paperback and note what time it is on the clock on the wall, the address, the weather, and a brief description of what Marc and Kathy were wearing. Then, slowly, tentatively you lead me down the hall. You look back at me and put a finger to your lips and shhhh me. You don't think I know what this means but you do it anyway. You smile at me as I yawn in response. Very carefully you approach the door and give me the hand signal to lie down. You smile again when I lie down. You look to the left to see if anyone is coming down the hallway and then look to the right, even though there's just a wall at the other end. Then you take the glass out of your tote-bag dramatically. You are trying not to make a sound of any kind. You do not want the glass to brush the fabric or for the bag to brush against a wall. You take the glass and ever so softly press it to the door and press your ear against it. You ignore me as I cock my head to the side, look up and watch you. You stare blankly as you listen.

But daddy, I don't want you to ache down there anymore.

You look down at me and then stare, emotionless down the hallway again. You hear someone talking approaching the entry to the hallway so you pull the glass away, quickly hide it behind me and slowly start to kneel down as if taking off my leash. When they pass by, you stand up quickly, grabbing the glass in one motion and then deliberately press it to the door again. You are too good at this. You press your ear and hear nothing but the sound of Kathy moaning with something in her mouth. You think you hear Marc panting or groaning low but then, you think, it could be a fan or the air-conditioning turning on. You look up and notice there are no vents near us in the hallway. You press your ear back to the glass again and hear Marc saying,

That's right, bend over like you're picking your toys.

You hear Kathy say,

Daddy, make me feel better.

Okay baby, just like the other times.

You stare blankly ahead. Your face registers nothing. You

do not blink. You do not wet your lips. You just listen. You don't even imagine, just listen. You hear the words. You know what they mean. You know what is happening. You know what no one else knows because you listen.

Daddy, something is shooting in me again,

you hear Kathy say, mildly out of breath. You are hard in your pants. You look down at me as if to see if I know that you are hard in your pants. You know that I know that you are hard. You know that I can smell you sweating. You wonder if I can smell Marc's sweat, and Kathy's sweat, and Kathy's wet cunt, and Marc's warm cum in Kathy's wet cunt. You look at me and I know that's what you're thinking. I can.

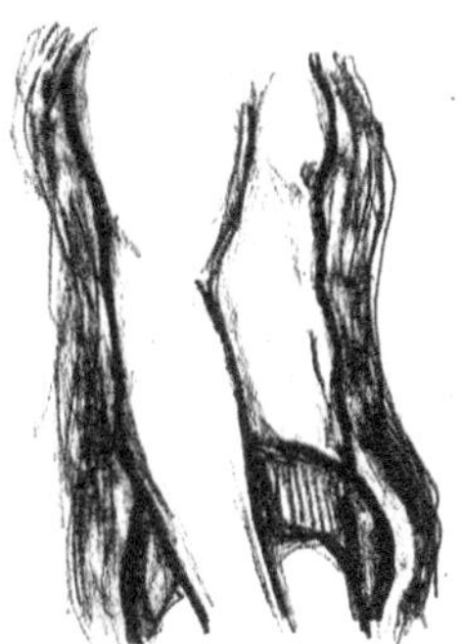

Wanting to be pure love is always just a tantrum, Kathy thinks. But pure ego is pure pain. She heard the part about ego at a new age seminar given by a rabbi who was also a sex offender. The man was really just saying things but the part about pain was true. I am the least enlightened person in the world, Kathy thinks. She starts laughing. Marc is at work. She walks around his apartment, which is her apartment now, too, and starts walking faster around the apartment, and is sort of skipping around the apartment thinking that she isn't enlightened at all. She thinks teevee is the new meditation, which is funny to her, and walks to the corner store and buys an iced coffee. It is very warm out. Kathy is wearing denim shorts and Marc's t-shirt. Her hair is piled on top of her head in a bun. She isn't wearing any makeup. She sort of feels like she has a good body. She doesn't feel particularly smart but she doesn't feel stupid either. She thinks

I love Marc,

and then she wonders if she does and then she thinks it doesn't matter much. She goes to the newsstand and buys some fashion magazines. She walks back to the apartment and sits on the terrace in the sun and looks at magazines. She folds down the corners on pages that picture items she wants to purchase. She doesn't know if she'll actually purchase them because she isn't a particularly organized person. She and Kim send text messages back and forth. Kathy tells Kim that she is in a serious relationship. Kim texts

fuck you

then texts

I love you.

Kathy texts back

shut up I love you.

Kim texts

visit soon.

Kathy texts

I will.

When Kathy was a teenager, she listened to music on an early version of the iPod while she walked to school or rode the bus. She imagined the songs she listened to were a soundtrack and played out parts of her life as movies in her head. The movies were highly fictionalized and sometimes she was basically someone else. If she was in a good mood, she listened to dance music or upbeat rock and roll music and was the heroine. If she was depressed, she listened to Bright Eyes and Elliot Smith and killed herself in the movie or stared at things blankly. In college, Kathy told a friend that she had done this in high school. The friend admitted to having done the same thing. Kathy mentioned it to more friends and many of them had done the same or similar or related in some way.

When Kathy was a kid, she wanted to be a glamorous housewife like her mother, or else a movie star. Kathy was an okay actress but she lost the drive to pursue it before she had a good enough body that it might have been possible. Other girls thought their mothers were glamorous and realized later that their mothers were average. Kathy's mother was, in reality, very glamorous. She was very judgmental and vain but she loved Kathy and was a good mother as much as anyone can be a good mother. She wanted Kathy to be a housewife, though she would never tell Kathy this, because being a housewife meant reading books all day and taking not-for-credit courses at the university and travelling and writing letters and talking on the telephone and shopping and having parties and going out to lunch. Kathy's mother read everything and was conscious of how she was perceived. Kathy's mother was the subject of dislike sprung from the jealousy of other women. All men liked
85→ Kathy's mother. Women were jealous of Kathy's mother because she was pretty and had excellent haircuts and was generally glamorous and didn't have to work and never got in fights with her husband because she knew how to handle men. She warned Kathy that women would be jealous of her.

Women are jealous of us because we are pretty and because we don't care very much what they think of us and we are not worried if they will like us or not. If a woman is smart she won't be jealous of us because she won't waste her time with that kind of feeling.

Kathy's mother wasn't at all cold. She was a kind woman who volunteered for human rights campaigns and progressive political candidates. Kathy's mother was a very feeling woman. Kathy is a very feeling woman, but she doesn't have any children and she feels like she's suffered enough. It's fall and then it's winter and Kathy wants to have a warm enough coat and keep the heat on all the time. Kathy doesn't want to be bohemian and she doesn't want to be poor and she doesn't want to be on hard drugs. Kathy buys Marc a giant teevee for Christmas with Marc's money. Marc is happy with the teevee and says they will watch movies together. Marc gives Kathy an engagement ring. He asks her in a minimally dramatic way if she would like to get married and she says sure. Kathy and Marc watch *White Christmas* on the new teevee. Marc doesn't mind when Kathy talks over the movie. Marc isn't home much because he works a lot. Kathy doesn't mind him being gone most of the time. She feels happy to see him when he comes home. She likes looking at her engagement ring. She gets regular manicures.

There are no first acts in American life. It never begins. My mother moved me into the cities as I slept inside of her.   It is always so cold in the cities. Everything is steel and loss. I kissed the post of a traffic light once. I drank a bottle of Prosecco by myself and took two ecstasy. I guess I was wilder in college. In the asphalt, I am home.   The twenty-four hour news cycle is the last remaining sacrament in American life. It is the final sanctuary of attention, the last vestige of the bicameral mind.   I'd read a newspaper if I could find one. Sunday morning. With tobacco. And Irish coffee. Mistrustful, lazy, and discontent.   The other day I was reading the letters between Jefferson and Adams where they discussed religion. We live in a generation of zealots. The most offensive are the zealots who genuflect before nothing. Supplicate themselves before nothing. They are slaves. We are free. Or vice versa.   Before noon, I'll have two dates for that evening. I'll invite them both to the same tacky bistro and sit across from them at a table with the red and white checkered tablecloth. Real Italian, I'll tell them. I'll stare at them deliberately, unwaveringly and tell them: before you is a man on whom you cannot rely.   At home I'll put my feet up on the coffee table and Kathy will mutter something into the phone. She holds it to her head with her shoulder while looking at something on her iPad. I forgot to take my shoes off.   Sometimes, when it is still gray out I go for runs in the park. I duck into the bushes and piss there. I drink my water bottle in one gulp. I see the same painfully thin and painfully fat women, the same self-obsessed men. I sit on a bench and smoke a cigarette and think,

This is what it has come to. We have sat, an easy generation, in houses
87→ thought to be indestructible.

That's why we built all those tall boxes in Manhattan and those thin aerials that amuse the Atlantic swell.   I feel nothing but the wind. And hunger. I am satisfied with the absence and the silence. I know that I am renting this space in the morning. I am leasing each exhalation. And after us there will be nothing worth talking about.   In the earthquakes to come, and there will be earthquakes, I very much hope that I will have one final drink, one final cigarette, and someone by my side. Someone that will weep for my death far more than they will mourn their own. I meant to pack a lunch. I meant to take some things with me. I meant to write you a list. Let you know what to save. You can stay behind if you want. Just don't leave me. I don't want to be alone. Until I'm with you. Then I want the whole world to melt away and take you with it. What a coincidence.

www.ingramcontent.com/pod-product-compliance
Lightning Source LLC
Chambersburg PA
CBHW030428310726
48979CB00009B/1664/J

9789198090321